GREAT
RESCUES

JOHN THOMAS CROWLEY

Order of Characters

Anjala
Hamish
Emerita
Dantel
Priya

Also by John Thomas Crowley

Brilliant Challenges
Meeting V.I.Ps
The Smart Kids

ANJALA

Home for Anjala and her brother Rajesh was a small, snow-covered village high in the Himalayan Mountains of the tiny Kingdom of Nepal. In the valley below lay the small town of Pokhara, where she and her brother attended school most days. The daily treks back and forth to school along the narrow and dangerous mountain paths were challenging, but to two Nepalese children this was the norm.

The classroom clock that hung above the board was showing 3.15pm and in a few minutes the bell would go, bringing the school day to a close. Anjala looked out of the window; the January snowstorm that had been raging all day had abated. The fresh snow that had covered the area meant it would be impossible for her and Rajesh, along with the other schoolchildren that came from the surrounding villages, to attempt the journey home. A simple text from her mother confirmed that she and Rajesh were to spend the next few days with their aunt, who lived in a large flat above one of the many ironmongers' shops scattered around the town.

Outside the air had a chilling nip to it; while waiting for Rajesh she looked up at the sparkling, snow-covered mountains, now set against a deep blue sky. The powdered snow that had recently come to rest on the summit's peaks of the Annapurna range was now being blown around by savage, vicious winds; plumes of what appeared to be white dust could clearly be seen spiralling high into the atmosphere.

Leaning against the school gate post, Anjala wondered how her snow leopard, whom she had named Heaven, and her cub had coped with the recent blizzards. Her train of thought was broken by the boisterous eruption of Rajesh and his mates from the classroom.

"What were you thinking about, Anjala?" asked Rajesh.

"I was thinking about Heaven and her cub."

"Who's Heaven?" asked one of Rajesh's mates.

"None of your business," snarled Anjala, for she knew what the villagers' reaction would be if they found out a snow leopard was prowling the area. Anjala had learnt from her school teacher that the snow leopard was an elusive creature and would avoid human contact at all cost, but a mother with a hungry cub may be tempted by an easy kill. The villagers' livestock would be a soft target for a powerful snow leopard like Heaven. Would Heaven attack if desperate? Most likely. This was a chance Anjala couldn't take. She understood why the locals would want to protect their animals at any cost; they were poor people living a simple life and the loss of one of their herd or flock was a loss of income they could ill afford. Both she and Rajesh knew they had to keep Heaven and her cub's whereabouts a secret.

As Anjala walked with her brother to her Aunt's flat she remembered the day they first saw Heaven and her cub; it was early October. Her father, to support the family income, helped out in the main trekking season as a Sherpa. He had heard that a small team of American climbers needed the knowledge of local Sherpas to guide them over the Annapurna Mountains but, more importantly, to assist them with climbing Machapuchare, more commonly known as Fishtail. The climbers had been given consent by the Nepalese authorities to climb the mountain with the strict instruction not to ascend the summit. Fishtail is a sacred peak in the Hindu religion associated with the God Shiva. Lord Shiva is supposed to live on the peak. The climbers would pay handsomely, but an early start the next morning was needed.

Dawn had arrived and their father shouted at them to hurry up as he needed to be down the mountainside in Pokhara to meet the American expedition team. Their father set a fast pace, too fast for them, so they let him go ahead; she and Rajesh would slowly amble down looking at their phones as they went, checking to see what messages had been left and who was on Facebook. Turning the corner, there in front of them was one of the world's most elusive big cats. A female snow leopard. Anjala recalled how Rajesh froze with fear that morning and how her heart pounded to almost breaking point. Their father had told them how to react if they came across a snow leopard: remain calm and back away slowly, for they were powerful killers who commanded respect. The likelihood of encountering such a majestic animal as the snow leopard would be extremely slim, but nevertheless treat with caution. Heaven merely stopped in her tracks. Her pale green eyes gave a fleeting glance in their direction; her light smoke-grey coat with its black open rosettes and spots made her a master of disguise, blending in beautifully with the colours of the surrounding rocks. Moments later she had vanished, melting into the natural habitat as she bounded back up the mountain.

Over the past few months, tension in the mountain villages had grown as more and more villagers reported losses and attacks on their livestock, and that snow leopard tracks had been found. Anjala kept quiet about Heaven.

In the depths of the Nepalese winter, Anjala and Rajesh had more sightings of Heaven and recently her new cub, which was now three to four months old and fresh out of the den. It was normal for snow leopards to come down from the high peaks to lower terrain in the winter months, but this brought them into contact with mankind and the inevitable tensions and conflicts that followed. Anjala had come up with the idea of leaving food out each night near the place where she and Rajesh had first encountered Heaven, the hope being if it was Heaven attacking the villagers' livestock to provide food for herself and her cub this would stop the attacks and the tensions within the villages and maybe spare her life. For a few weeks the trick worked, but stealing meat several times a week from the local meat stores in Pokhara was risky and would no doubt get her and Rajesh into trouble. The risk of getting caught increased as the weeks went by; one afternoon on the way home from school a meat store holder caught them in the act and released his dogs to give chase. They ran for their lives, but as they sprinted down the street they dropped the bag of meat and the dogs were distracted by the bag, giving her and Rajesh extra time to make their getaway. That afternoon was a narrow escape for Anjala and Rajesh and they took the decision to abandon their stealing adventures. They would have to come up with another plan.

Breakfast the next morning was a simple affair and was quickly put away. Walking to school with Rajesh a few paces behind her, being the grumpy brother as usual, Anjala spotted her father in one of the local cafés drinking tea with a small group of her village elders. She pushed the café door open, gave her father a hug and asked what the occasion was. "No occasion," her father said, but fresh tracks had been found on the edge of the village; they belonged to a female snow leopard and a cub, plus more livestock had been attacked and killed last night. Anjala's heart sank but she tried not to show it.

"What do you propose to do, father?"

"We propose to get permission to track the snow leopard down and shoot her."

Anjala's father looked at his daughter's face and read her distraught feelings.

"Sometimes, Anjala, we have to do unpleasant things, and this is one of those occasions. We must protect the village and our livestock; you know that we need to keep the animals safe so that we can sell them. I know the snow leopard is doing what she needs to do to survive for herself and her cub, but we need to survive as well. Do you see my point?"

"Yes, father."

Anjala ran out of the café, glancing up and down the street looking for Rajesh. Crossing the road, barely avoiding being run over by a school bus, she stopped to see if Rajesh was in sight. Four blocks down she caught a glimpse of her brother's blue sports bag; he had managed to meet up with some of his classmates. She pushed people out of her way as she tried to catch up with him. The traffic lights at the top of the street were green so the pedestrians had to wait. What felt like ages was only a matter of a few minutes before the lights changed in her favour. As she fidgeted around she happened to give a cursory look into the internet café; there was the Australian film crew all her friends had been talking about. Rumour had it they had come to make a documentary about snow leopards but, like most film crews, the creature had eluded them and they were going home empty-handed. She recalled her teacher one day talking about the various film crews that came to town and that their aim was to educate the world about the animals they filmed and how best to protect them from man's needs. Hastily she put two and two together. She needed their expertise in protecting Heaven and her cub, and they needed snow leopards.

Cautiously pushing the door aside she entered the internet café; the guys were busy downloading information for something she didn't understand.

"Excuse me," she spluttered.

"Yes, sweetheart?" A lady from the crew replied.

Anjala cleared her throat and started to tell the crew about her snow leopard Heaven and her cub, along with all the issues that had happened recently and what the outcome would be.

The hot chocolate drink and lemon drizzle cake she had been offered were wonderful; for a poor Nepalese mountain girl a treat of this kind was rare, and she appreciated the gesture, but there was work to be done.

The lady film director couldn't believe her luck and insisted Anjala call her Elizabeth. A plan of action had been briefly scribbled on a napkin, but Anjala was to call her father and the village elders for talks. She sent a text to her brother.

'Be here in five minutes.'

The plan was as follows:

- Anjala and Rajesh would show the film crew Heaven and her cub's hiding places; in return the film company in charge would pay the village a handsome reward for gaining access to the snow leopards.
- Anjala and Rajesh would be in the film documentary to tell their story.
- A conservation team would be set up, providing better fences to protect the villagers' livestock.
- Infrared remote cameras would be set up on all tracks/routes the snow leopards used

during darkness. The villagers could check the cameras every day and if Heaven or any other snow leopard triggered the cameras into action near the village, then the villages could take the appropriate action – mainly post lookouts to scare the cats away.

- The cameras would also allow the conservationists to study and monitor the snow leopards' activities so that more could be learnt about the habits of this great elusive cat.
- The village elders would organise official trekking expeditions so that tourists could come and learn about Heaven or other snow leopards in their natural surroundings.

Anjala thought the plan was excellent. The organised walks would bring in much needed income for the village, as foreign visitors would pay for an organised trip to see and learn more about the snow leopards. She and Rajesh could open a small café serving light refreshments; the money they made would go into the village money pot.

"Father, this is a win-win situation; the village gets more protection, a better warning system and a much needed income source. Plus Heaven and her cub will have a brighter future, as the villagers will see the snow leopards as an income source to be protected rather than as a threatening menace to their livestock."

Her father looked at her.

"Father, you know this is the right way forward."

"Anjala, we need to look at all the options and think what is right for the villagers and the snow leopards. This will take time, but we, the elders, will grant that time. For the moment make sure Heaven stays away from our livestock. But for now, both of you get to school."

"Yes, father," replied Anjala and Rajesh.

The sprint to school made them just in time for the first lesson of the day. Anjala sat at her desk and looked out of the same window she had done yesterday afternoon; the snow had started to come down again. She could see her village high up in the mountains, the peak of Fishtail in the background and somewhere, roaming the mountain slopes, was her Heaven and her cub, safe with a brighter future thanks to what she had achieved earlier.

A text appeared on her phone.

'Why do you call your snow leopard Heaven?'

It was from her father. She replied:

'Simple father, she comes down from the mountain peaks high in the heavens at dusk and goes back up to the mountain summits in the heavens at dawn, so I called her Heaven. See you soon x.'

Another text message appeared on her phone; it was from Elizabeth, the film director. They had managed to obtain some funding from the World Wildlife Fund; these funds would allow new programmes to be put in place so as to demonstrate to the world that, with careful management, wildlife and humans could exist alongside each other, bringing benefits to all concerned. For a few moments Anjala thought the message was interesting but couldn't understand the relevance to her: it wasn't until she scrolled down and she saw the invitation for herself and Rajesh to go to Australia to present the programme to schools all over Australia. Anjala's eyes lit up with the thought of going to Australia; she and her brother had never gone further than a few day trips to Kathmandu, the capital of Nepal. She had been to Tribhuvan Airport, Nepal's main international Airport on the outskirts of Kathmandu, several times as her uncle often flew out to Doha in Qatar to work on the building sites there; but she never in her wildest dreams envisaged flying out to an exotic location herself. She called her brother, but he didn't respond as usual, so she sent a message to his Facebook page; he constantly kept an eye on that. As predicted the response was immediate: *'OMG, will father let us go?'*

In her excitement Anjala had not considered that small matter; a dark horizon clouded her judgement for a few short minutes. Surely he would let them go? As she walked up the narrow mud track, a path she had trampled along hundreds of times, she pondered on how she would delicately place the proposition to her father. She looked up at the mountains that soared above her – the snow on the Annapurna peaks that dominated the skyline was being blown around high into the stratosphere, nightfall would soon descend and the street lights of Pokhara far below would soon twinkle, adding a magic charm of its own to the valley she had known as home.

The flight from Kathmandu via New Delhi in India to Perth, Australia was long and exhausting but exciting. For Anjala and her brother Rajesh every minute of this four-week adventure would be relished and remembered for years to come. Their father had reluctantly agreed, proving the strategy she had shrewdly hatched out on the trek home that late winter's afternoon had worked. Her plan was heavily weighted on emphasizing to her father that he was vital to this project and that he was included in the trip to Australia. Getting Elizabeth to visit her father and the other village elders on numerous occasions, reassuring them of her and Rajesh's safety, had also worked in tipping the balance in her favour. Stressing the trip would be a very good educational experience also added bonus points in her direction. Anjala was quite proud of her cunning prowess. Offering money to support the village funds as a little sweetener had also improved the odds. A sneaky little bribe – or so called inducement – with a nod and a wink in the right place sometimes gets the job done.

The temperature outside the main air-conditioned terminal buildings was a staggering forty degrees. As Anjala stepped out of the confines of the airport buildings the heat hit her in the face. It was winter back home but, here in Australia, it was the middle of summer. Snow leopards do not live in Australia. They belong to the mountains of the Himalayas. Australia was the land of kangaroos, wallabies, kookaburras, koala bears and other indigenous species.

The schedule was going to be busy; over twenty schools across Australia would be visited from Queensland to New South Wales to here in Western Australia. Anjala and her brother would face the students and through an interpreter explain how their snow leopard, Heaven, and her cub, who survive on the edge of life, had been saved/rescued from the hands of the village elders as a result of putting in place a more effective early warning system, notifying the villages as to Heaven's whereabouts within the vicinity. This would ensure an appropriate course of action was taken to scare her off as opposed to killing her. Better fences had been built around the villages. Anjala explained at each school that the initial money to put the necessary defences in place came from the TV company who had organised their trip here. Money to maintain the programme would come from tourists, who were eager to learn about the ways and lives of the snow leopard and prepared to pay for organised tours run by the villagers. Rajesh went on to say killing the leopards to protect the village livestock would have a knock-on effect; no snow leopards, no tourists, no income. Anjala continued the theme, saying this simple and effective programme can be adapted to protecting and rescuing other threatened wildlife in the world. To protect or rescue our wildlife from extinction you have to address the local issues that are the root causes in bringing about the decline in some of our wildlife populations. Poverty is one of the underlying factors; if your livelihood is being threatened by the natural world that exists around you, it isn't unreasonable for that community to take whatever measures it needs to protect itself, and that very often means the demise of the local wildlife. A wild animal protecting its food source would do exactly the same. There is no point tutting at the TV from the comfort of your own home condemning others who live desperate, precarious lives; you have to understand their situation and solve those issues before you can instigate a suitable programme to ensure endangered species like our snow leopard, Heaven, stand a chance of surviving this cut-throat rat race of a world we live in.

The schools Anjala and Rajesh visited were quite receptive to what they had to say; some of the schools had begun adopting their own individual projects to support the wildlife in their local area. Briefly Anjala and Rajesh had become mini celebs, as TV companies and newspapers phoned asking for interviews and inviting them into their studios. They had caught the attention of the Australian media and the short spell of being in the public limelight was powerful and exciting. The chat show hosts and the newspaper hacks were genuinely interested in their story. All the talks they had given had been well-documented and a mini TV series that tracked their every move over the last few weeks would be screened to the various world networks in a few months' time. Hopefully their story will have an impact and start to make other children around the world stop and think about the environment around them and what they could do. You never know; young teenagers from around the globe just might lift their heads from the contents of their smartphones and look to see what is happening around them. For Anjala and Rajesh, seeing new parts of the world and being newfound celebs had certainly opened their eyes and the thought of making new documentaries about the plight of the planet's wildlife in other parts of the world was enticing. Anjala could envisage herself being a social media superstar like Kim Kardashian! Wow, wouldn't she be rich! No more poverty and having to live in a tin hut with a blue corrugated roof, twelve thousand feet up a cold Himalayan mountain. But for the time being it was the long flight home.

The arrivals lounge at Tribhuvan Airport on the outskirts of Kathmandu was crowded with paparazzi. Emerging from customs via the sliding doors, Anjala and Rajesh were greeted by a wall of flashing photographers and news hacks thrusting microphones in their faces. Their story had gone viral. Rajesh was overwhelmed with all the media attention, but Anjala was only just getting started with a new life she was beginning to relish. Their mother was at the far end of the arrivals hall – the look on her face didn't exactly exude a glow of joy, quite the opposite in fact. The words back to school tomorrow for you two, uttered by her mother as they got into a waiting taxi, kind of brought Anjala back to reality; her fledgling career of being a world superstar just might have to be put on the back burner for a while. But not for long; she would work on her strategy over the next few weeks.

HAMISH

The school summer holidays in Scotland were drawing to an end; Hamish and his friends Ceardach and Niall had spent the last remaining days up in the moorlands tracking the red deer. They had built a small hideout from local stones, which they had managed to scavenge from the dry stone builders' yard at the end of the village. The hidey-hole was a perfect watchtower, particularly as they had managed to blend it into the natural surroundings by throwing purple heather and fallen tree branches from the nearby forest over the top.

Hamish had become attached to a magnificent fourteen pointer stag, which he named Rufus; this was a royal stag getting ready for probably his last autumn rut. Ceardach's mother had told them that any stag with more than twelve points on his antlers was deemed a royal stag and would be a highly prized trophy for the deer stalkers.

The late warm summer days attracted the horrible biting midges and staying in the hideout was uncomfortable, so Hamish and his friends often spent their time playing on the open moorland in full view of Rufus and his hinds. Taking turns to play Laird of the Manor was a favourite pasttime, but often ended up in a glorious fight as each vied to be the Laird and boss the others around. The great stag would watch the goings-on from a safe distance, but as the days went by he encroached ever nearer. Hamish and his friends got more excited as the big stag came closer to them. Ceardach had worked out that Rufus had become accustomed to their presence and didn't see them as a threat.

Niall's father was the estates manager for the local highland estate and on several occasions that summer he had spent the day following in his father's footsteps around the farm; he knew where the feedstock and estate machinery were kept and which drawer in his father's office the various keys to the outbuildings were kept. A thought occurred to him – putting feed out around the hideout would attract the stag, and that in turn would score him brownie points with Hamish and Ceardach, but first he needed to get his hands on the keys. He knew stealing the keys for a few hours would raise suspicion, but if he could get an imprint of the required key by pressing it into some Plasticine, that would solve the matter. All he had to do was bide his time and wait for an opportune moment. The ideal occasion arose one afternoon when the estate gillie accidentally dropped a bunch of keys on the office floor. Niall recognised the feed store key instantly; dashing across the office he grabbed the keys, turning to face the wall so nobody could see what he was up to. Taking the plasticine from his top pocket he quickly made an impression before turning to face the estate gillie and hand the keys back, making it look like he was being helpful. With the key imprint he dashed out of the office door.

"Where are you going, Niall?" shouted Miss

Turner, one of the estate office clerks.

"I'll be back shortly."

"You better, your father has asked us to look after you."

With that statement ringing in his ears, Niall was off to see the local village locksmith.

"I'm back, Miss Turner."

"Thank goodness for that, your father has told us all off for letting you go."

"Don't worry about that, Miss Turner, I'll tell him it was my fault and that I was in a rebellious mood. He'll believe that."

"What's in the bag, Niall?" enquired Hamish.

"Feedstock."

"Whatever for?" asked Ceardach.

Niall explained his reasoning and how he got access to the feed shed.

"Niall, you are a genius." screamed Hamish.

Brownie points at last, thought Niall.

"Quick march." barked Hamish and, with that order, all three headed off to the hideout.

Hamish couldn't get over Niall's ingenuity; the rutting season started in a few weeks and Rufus would need all the food source he could get to make sure he had enough energy to sustain him in the forthcoming fights he would face to protect his harem of hinds from other stags and get mating access to the hinds.

Ceardach knew that the ideal opportunity to observe the deer feeding would be early dawn. With this fact in mind, Hamish and his friends set their alarm clocks for early the next morning.

The sight that greeted them as they approached the hidey-hole was a dream to behold. There in the swirl of the morning mist, in amongst the hinds, was Rufus the royal stag. As the boys approached Rufus cautiously stepped forward, as if to protect the hinds. Hamish walked towards him. His heart was pounding; for a split second he thought his heart would burst. The great stag sniffed at the boys. Niall quietly bent down and scraped a few pellets into his hands, and with quivering arms he reached out to Rufus. To all of their amazement Rufus stepped forward and delicately nibbled at the feed in Niall's hand. Hamish could not believe his eyes; this magnificent royal stag he had named Rufus was standing directly in front of him. He stared at his antlers and counted all fourteen points. He reached out to touch Rufus and as he did so the great stag lowered his head and all three boys were able to stroke his antlers. At that moment one of the hinds gave the alarm call and within an instant the whole herd disappeared into the morning mist.

"Wow!" said Ceardach.

Hamish swiftly turned to his friends. "We must not tell anyone about this."

As they returned to the village, only Mrs Mackay, the proprietor of the village store and Post Office, spotted the boys. "Where have you three been at this hour of the morning?"

"Oh, out for a walk, Mrs Mackay," spluttered Hamish.

"A likely story indeed, Hamish McTuff. Does

your mother know that you have been out on the moor this hour of the morning?"

"Ohoooo."

"I'll take that as a no, Hamish. Well, there is fresh bread and jam on the table in the back room; go on in and have some breakfast, all of you. You look as if you've all seen a ghost. A good mug of tea will put the colour back in all of your cheeks."

Ceardach picked up the local morning paper that was on the table next to the large brown teapot. The headlines read: *'Millionaire Businessman finds Royal Stag.'* With horror he read on; an organised shoot on the nearby highland estate for corporate companies from London had attracted many wealthy clients. The shoot was starting today; many of the clients had already been out on the moors with the local gamekeepers over the past few days establishing their prime positions.

The boys looked at each other; they knew Rufus was an old stag past his best and under the culling guidelines for the stags at this time of the year he would be a prized trophy. His hinds would be safe from the stalker's guns, as it was out of season for them. They had to think fast. Niall had an idea; his father had an old quad bike that was kept in the shed at the bottom of their garden. He knew where the keys would be, plus having been taught to drive it by his older brother without his parent's knowledge at the age of ten last year just might come in useful at this precise moment. Having polished off Mrs Mackay's offered breakfast, leaving only crumbs and a thin layer of jam at the bottom of the jar, they snuck out the back door with a plan in place.

Hamish and Ceardach would head straight back to the hideout; while Niall would get his father's quad bike and meet them there shortly.

Hamish stopped halfway down the road.

"Now what are we stopping for?" asked Ceardach.

"Never mind, go to the hidey-hole," snapped Hamish as he retraced his tracks and headed home. As he sprinted up the last fifty metres of the dirt track that led to his front door, Hamish frantically tried to remember the safe combinations; he looked at the keypad on his smartphone and tried to envisage the codes he had seen on a tatty piece of paper with his father's scribbled handwriting on. Hamish had discreetly watched his father key in the new codes the other night as he placed a medium-sized dark grey plastic case in it. The safe was one of the old cast-iron affairs and sat in the corner of his father's study, which was at the far end of the outbuilding at the back of the house. The key to the study was always kept under a loose floorboard in the spare bedroom. Hamish's father had made it perfectly clear on numerous occasions to him and his mother that neither of them should go in there under any circumstances. That was his father's territory. His father was a Major in the armed services seconded to reconnaissance duties for the past twelve months; the missions he went on were top secret and, judging by the winter clothing that was piled up in the utility room,

Hamish and his mother had surmised that his last mission, which he had returned from the other night, was Russia.

At breakfast yesterday morning, his father took an urgent call; his briefcase was on the table and as he got up to take the call he closed the lid down but didn't shut the case completely. Hamish sneaked around the kitchen table and, slowly lifting the lid, peeked in to his father's briefcase. On top was a Military & Government brochure about a SkyRanger, a top of the range model. To Hamish this was a super drone or Quad copter; whatever the difference, if there was such a difference. Wow, he thought!! He'd love to have a go on that; his own Quad copter/drone his father bought him last year was a quality model but nowhere near as sophisticated as the one in his father's safe. His he operated from an app on his smartphone; tilting the phone would alter the flight path of the drone. Hamish was intrigued as to how this super drone worked; reaching across the table for his iPhone he quickly photographed the brochure. He felt like an international spy photographing top classified documents. He was careful to make sure the brochure was in exactly the same position as he placed it back in his father's briefcase as it was when he lifted it out; his father, being a military man, had an acute sense of attention to detail and would notice the brochure had been tampered with straight away and he would be severally reprimanded, punished by means of a week's grounding with no access to his laptop or phone.

Every young person's nightmare.

Hamish cast a cursory glance at the SkyRanger's specs; he was amazed to see that the flight time was up to fifty minutes and that it would stay airborne in gusty wind speeds of up to fifty miles per hour and that it could ascend up to an altitude of fifteen hundred feet with a beyond line-of-sight range of three miles. Usual facts, he thought. He looked at how easy and fast it was to assemble and was suitably impressed with its ability to take off and land vertically. Getting used to the intuitive interface pad that controlled and directed the drone would take a little time to master, but with plenty of practise he could soon overcome those issues. If only he could get his greedy, grubby little hands on it.

Hamish looked at the most recent messages on his phone; among them was a message from his mother saying that she and his father had gone to Aberdeen to do some shopping and would be back later in the afternoon. Hamish punched the air. "Yessss." He scrambled up the stairs and headed straight for the spare room; lifting the floorboard up, he lay flat on the floor and with his right arm he fumbled his way around under the floor, searching for the key. With the key in his hand and the loose floorboard put back in place he raced down the stairs, missing the odd step as he went along. Tearing across the garden he reached his father's study. Ben, the family's border collie, who was tethered to a nearby post, just looked on with amazement written in his eyes – he had never seen Hamish move with such speed and urgency. Hamish crouched down to the safe; he was reasonably confident that he knew the code to the top combination, and he knew the small keys to the combination locks were in the small red tin cashbox that sat on the top shelf, and the key to that box was at the bottom of the blue tin mug that had all his father's pens and pencils in next to the twenty seven inch screen iMac. Scrambling both combination locks, he lined the zero on both dials to the red line on the outer circumference. Working the top combination first he twisted the dial in an anticlockwise movement, stopping at the right number on the fifth turn; twisting the dial in an alternating fashion between anticlockwise and clockwise movements he stopped at the last number. If the code was right, with a further alternate twist, the dial would lock into position. With bated breath he gave a final twist of the dial, and mercifully it clicked into the locked position. Now for the bottom combination; this was going to take some huge imagination and thinking. He would have to get into his father's mind-set. The small clock that hung on the study back wall showed the time as 10am – time was against him, the others would be wondering where he was. He made several attempts but the dial was not locking into position after the last number. Ben's barking was starting to annoy him, but something jogged his memory... Ben the dog! Why did his father ask his mother the other night for Ben's full date of birth and age? Hmm… he thought. He scrambled the dial for the last time, resetting to zero, and put Ben's information in. With a huge sigh of relief the dial locked into position; turning the handle down he pulled the safe door open and there was the SkyRanger.

Ceardach's face as Hamish tipped the contents of the grey plastic case all over the place was one of utter disbelief.

"What the heck is that?"

"It's a flying saucer! What do you think it is?"

"I don't know."

"It's a drone."

"Where did you get that from?"

"It's my father's! Never mind where it came from, Ceardach."

"I take it he knows nothing about this little jaunt of yours?"

"Course he doesn't."

"What are you going to do with it, Hamish?"

"Watch."

Hamish looked down the glen as he assembled the drone, paying careful attention to the minutest detail in the instruction manual that was in a buttoned sleeve on the inside of the case's lid. Speed was vital, as he could see the cars bringing the deer stalkers winding their way up the mountainside. Soon they would be in position and the shoot would be on.

Niall quickly sped up the glen; as agreed, Hamish would stay at the watchtower with the drone scouting the area. Ceardach would ride with Niall; with one hand around Niall's waist for supposed safety and clutching a walkie-talkie in the other, the pair set off, riding roughshod across the moor, waiting for Hamish's instruction.

Hamish tapped the screen on the tablet's interface, launching the drone vertically up to a thousand feet; he anxiously scanned the glen, sending the drone in numerous directions. It wasn't long before he could see Rufus on the screen; his stag was high on the opposing ridge. Tapping the tablet, Hamish sent the SkyRanger meandering down the glen. With pinpoint accuracy he could see the deerstalkers rapidly closing in on Rufus. He screamed into the walkie-talkie Niall had thrown at him a few moments ago, with Rufus' precise coordinates. Whipping out his smartphone, he took a picture of the image that was on the tablet's interface and sent an Instragam photo to Ceardach's phone along with a text message, as the message would create a ping and just might get Ceardach's attention above the noise of the quad bike's engine. Strangely enough Ceardach felt his phone vibrate in his pocket; hanging on for dear life to Niall with his left hand he reached into his top left hand pocket with his right hand. He glimpsed at the text and the Instagram photo; yelling at Niall at the top of his voice he screamed to stop for a moment. With the quad coming to an abrupt halt Ceardach shoved his phone in Niall's face. Both of them looked at the picture and instantly recognised the ridge. Like Hamish, they knew the glen like the back of their hands, the shortcuts and the pitfalls to avoid, but so did the gamekeepers escorting the deer stalkers. Ceardach could see Rufus in the distance; he goaded Niall to push the bike to its limit, but it was no use. The deer stalkers, with the estate's faster quads, had the advantage and soon they would be in position with their high velocity rifles to take aim and claim Rufus as a prized victory. The gamekeepers and the estate would receive their money. Niall snatched Ceardach's phone and sent a text message to Hamish. *'Buzz the herd with the drone. Scare them, but make sure you send them scattering up the glen on to the next estate. If Rufus is on the next Laird's land the gamekeepers will have no authority to follow.'*

A narrow, well-trodden track that the deer used to crisscross the purple and white heather lay to Niall and Ceardach's left. It was the quickest path to the stag, but they would have to continue their venture by foot. As they raced along the beaten track they began to scream and shout, waving their arms about in the vain attempt of spooking the deer. The trick had worked but unfortunately the panicked herd, with Rufus in the fore, headed down the glen in the wrong direction. The images the SkyRanger was sending back to the tablet in Hamish's hand were not encouraging; having sent the drone down the glen tracking the deer stalkers, he could see that they were all well-camouflaged and embedded in the moorland vegetation and that the gamekeepers were clearly agitated as their game plan, that had being meticulously worked upon over the recent days, had gone seriously awry. Hamish had picked up Niall's message – sweeping the drone back towards the panicked herd that was hurtling down the glen he dropped the SkyRanger's height to five feet. Encircling Rufus with the Quad copter appeared to temporarily confuse him – it did halt him in his tracks – but that wouldn't be for long. Hamish shouted at the top of his voice for Rufus to turn and head back up the glen, not that yelling would achieve much, as they were over half a mile apart, but it made him feel better.

All three boys had been well-versed by their fathers about the hazards of the outdoor life here on the highland moors, and that being fully prepared for all eventualities was not only wise but also vital. The Scottish highland weather had many moods and some of them were not pleasant. Niall reached into his rucksack that was on Ceardach's back. At the bottom, underneath his waterproof and torch, were the two red flares he had stolen from the estate's store room. Hamish could see that Rufus was standing still, as if transfixed to the ground; this was not a good position to be in nor was it part of the intended plan, as a stationary stag was a dead stag. Looking at the tablet's screen he tapped it, sending the drone back up in to the air, as it was apparent to Hamish that the SkyRanger buzzing around Rufus's head was not having the desired effect – quite the opposite in fact. The crack of a rifle reverberated across the glen. Hamish's heart sank but as he looked up he saw, to his horror, the SkyRanger imploding into the atmosphere, sending shards of debris into the azure sky. Two flares soared high across the glen, their red vapour trails crisscrossing the distant skyline as they continued their journey to nowhere. Hamish could only assume that one of his friends must have released the flares to scare Rufus and his hinds back to the ridge and in the direction of the next estate, where they would be safe as the gamekeepers and the trophy hunters had no licence to cull there.

The three boys had accomplished what they had set out to do, but the consequences of their actions would no doubt be swift and harsh. They would have to face the wrath of the estate managers and gamekeepers, whose pay would be less than expected. The royal stag had escaped their clutches.

For Niall, he would have to face his father for stealing the flares, the quad bike and embarrassing him in front of his wealthy clients that would have paid handsomely for this day's shoot; no doubt they would be looking for some kind of compensation that would cost the estate dearly.

As for Hamish, well, he had saved his fourteen pointer royal stag that he had got to know over the last few summer months. How he was going to justify his actions to his father he had no idea, nor was he looking forward to that conversation. The SkyRanger was military property; no doubt his father would have to face his bosses to give some kind of an explanation as to how military equipment entrusted into his care was utterly destroyed. Hamish was not looking forward to the punishment his father would no doubt mete out. Nevertheless, he had achieved his goal.

EMERITA

The small Swiss Alpine city of Davos lies near the southern German border. For Emerita and her three-year-old St Bernard rescue dog, Gretel, it was home. Mid-winter in the Alps meant deep snow and with that came the reality of avalanches, as layers of snow that had built up on the mountains over the harsh winter months became unstable, threatening to engulf everything that lay in their paths.

Emerita's house overlooked Davos; from her bedroom balcony she could see right across the valley that was spread out beneath her. The rooftops of the hotels, cafés, shops and churches that made up the small city were clothed in beautiful, soft glistening snow. The mountains in their splendid white winter coats looked majestic, but Emerita, like many of her friends, knew the hidden dangers that lay behind this picturesque setting.

Davos in the main was a quiet, backwater place, but for three days every year in late January, world political and business leaders from over a hundred countries came to discuss world issues. Emerita watched from her high vantage point as helicopters carrying world dignitaries landed at the various temporary heliports that had sprung up overnight. Her mother had told her what this year's theme was, but that was several days ago and, like any other twelve-year old girl, what her mother said normally went in one ear and straight out the other. Emerita looked around her room to see where she had put her laptop; clothes and shoes lay strewn all over the place. On the back of the door was a pinned message on bright yellow paper; the blue writing that had been hastily scribbled on it simply read:

'Tidy your room.'

Ignoring the message, she continued to scour her room. Gretel had taken her usual position on the bed. Emerita quickly realised that her laptop was embedded under Gretel, evidenced clearly by a white cable protruding from beneath her enormous head. She smartly pushed Gretel off her bed and, having retrieved the laptop, she logged on to the Internet with the aid of the house wi-fi, googling World Economic Forum Davos Switzerland. The Fourth Industrial Revolution meant nothing to her, but she did recall her brother Heinrich last night at dinner saying that this year's talks were all about building a better world for all. How? He wasn't sure, but it would involve improving technology and getting more people, particularly from poor countries, to use the internet. No doubt Heinrich would tell her more later, as he was working at the conference centre where the talks were being held.

Emerita continued to lie on her bed; logging on to her Facebook page she looked to see what her friends were up to. Gretel made herself known by placing a large paw gently on the duvet. Emerita looked at her best friend, whom she loved and adored; she could see from the look in Gretel's eyes the unceremonious way she had been dumped off the bed did not meet with approval. Standing a little less than a metre high, with one blue eye and one brown eye, she attempted to get back on the bed only to be rebuffed by Emerita. Her thick white coat with its deep chestnut-red patches was well suited to her surroundings, keeping her well insulated against the biting cold and making her visible in the snow blizzards that often raged for days on end in the high Alps in this mountainous region of Switzerland.

The cars bringing the delegates to the economic summit were lined up outside the conference centre, patiently waiting their turn to discharge the various world leaders. From her bedroom balcony vantage point Emerita could see the entire goings-on. The world's press were out in force, taking pictures of the rich and famous. The television on her bedroom wall had started to report that there had been an avalanche in the Davos Jacobshorn ski resort area and that a small group of cross-country skiers had been caught in the path of the avalanche and had been reported missing. A local TV company had managed to get footage of the avalanche as it happened from a skier who had videoed the event from her phone. Rumours had started to circulate that the wife of the French Ambassador to Germany was one of the skiers trapped.

Emerita's father flung open the door to her room. "We need to go."

He was reading a text message he had received

from the nearby mountain rescue team.

'All team members please report to the station immediately, we have received an urgent call requesting help to rescue a small party of cross-country skiers trapped by recent avalanche in the Davos Jacobshorn area.'

The rescue team managed by her father was often called out in the winter months to rescue skiers that had got into trouble; the call could come at any time and the team would have to be ready at a moment's notice. Having watched her father train and manage the team over the years, she opted to follow in his footsteps and had started her training last year. Her brother Heinrich had already started to train Gretel right from her early days as a fluffy young pup.

Gretel instinctively knew the call had come and was already outside pawing at the back of the four-wheel drive Jeep; en route she had picked up the traditional small wooden oak barrel that would hang round her neck, containing the all-important brandy synonymous with her breed and role in rescue. Emerita's father had already given instructions to a small helicopter crew. Within minutes the red helicopter of the rescue team had been scrambled and was airborne. On board, a doctor from the local hospital, along with two very experienced members of the team, were looking at their brief. Their job – explore the accident site, assess the situation and report back to Emerita's father.

The radio conversation with the pilot was short;

they had found the avalanche, the position was extremely dangerous and he would not be able to land the helicopter, so the rescue would have to be done on foot. The doctor and the other two members of the team were being winched down as they were speaking. The order was given by Emerita's father that the doctor and the other two were not to start the rescue mission until the full squad was assembled at the site.

Five minutes from receiving the call, the full team had assembled at the rescue station. Heinrich had already downloaded to everybody's phone maps of the area and made sure a paper version was in their rucksacks. With the team being fully briefed and everybody understanding their job, Emerita's father gave the go ahead to start the rescue. Emerita herself would take charge of Gretel, as Gretel was her dog.

The cable car station was only two blocks away on Bramabuelstrasse; Emerita had phoned the station warning them that they were on the way and to have a cable car available. The team loaded the cable car with all the equipment; Emerita sat quietly in the corner, keeping a watchful eye on Gretel and making sure she didn't jump up and down all over the place breaking the medical boxes or the important climbing gear. The Jacobshornbahn cable ride was split in two; at the halfway point at Ischalp they would have to switch cars, relocating all their stuff. As they ascended to the top, the cable car swayed as the wind buffeted it from all sides. The weather conditions had improved as the day went on; the snow blizzards that ushered in the day had given way to beautiful clear blue skies, creating the ideal setting for a good day's skiing. The avalanche unfortunately had put paid to that as the ski resorts suspended all activities. Emerita could see all the skiers heading back down the mountain to Davos, no doubt to the cafés and bars.

Gretel was getting excited; she could smell the snow and knew she was on an adventure. The doors of the cable car opened and a blast of ice-laced wind hit them all in the face. Emerita knew the first rules of any rescue; listen to the person in charge and follow instructions to the letter. Confirmation had filtered through that the cross-country skiers were a party of three, and that the French Ambassador to Germany had confirmed that his wife was in that small party, along with two members of his staff. The team got their apparatus ready; Emerita's father had taken the decision to rope Emerita to himself, as she was an inexperienced climber. Word had got around as to what had happened and that a rescue team was on its way. A rather large gentleman approached the squad and briefly explained who he was and that the cross-country party had only ventured out for a brief few hours' exercise and that they were experienced mountaineers. They were travelling light but had taken the minimal necessary essentials. "We have some clothing items in the rucksacks over there belonging to our friends; perhaps the dog could get scent markings?" Emerita dashed to the rucksacks and rummaged around, pulling out various designer T-shirts; she whistled to Gretel and wrapped the T-shirts around her nose, taking care to make sure Gretel got a good sniff of each item. The perfume on the French Ambassador's wife's clothes was very distinctive and no doubt expensive. Emerita knew how many hours of training her brother Heinrich had put into training Gretel for an event like this, particularly around looking for hidden objects by following the scent trail. St Bernards had been known to sniff bodies out that had been buried under three metres of snow.

Gretel's tail was up; she was raring to go. Despite being Emerita's dog, Heinrich had done all the training, so he rightly took the lead with Gretel close to his side. Eight members of the team followed, Emerita still roped to her father. The narrow track that led them to the avalanche site was treacherous. The whole team walked in silence so as to hear the slightest call for help. All eyes were peeled to the snowy slopes looking for any visible signs that could possibly indicate a fresh avalanche was imminent.

Forty minutes had passed since they had left the cable car; Heinrich spotted the other members of the rescue team who had been winched down by the helicopter over an hour ago, their bright orange coats plain to see. Emerita could see the extent of the avalanche and for a few seconds thought to herself, the cross-country skiers must be dead. She had never experienced the full force of an avalanche, but she had listened to people's personal ordeals and the stories they told about the velocity of the cascading snow and ice with all the debris trapped within, the deafening noise as thousands of tonnes of white stuff hurled down the mountainside and the swirling winds that sucked up everything in its path. She had seen the body bags that contained the corpses of those who hadn't survived past avalanches laid out on the floor of the rescue station. She had also seen the broken bodies of survivors taking months to heal. She knew the dangers that confronted her as she stood patiently waiting for her father's orders.

Emerita's father had listened to his team and had decided that the best course of action was to let Gretel do what she was trained to do. Freed to do her job, Gretel set to work sniffing the freshly-strewn snow. Hours passed, and with nightfall fast approaching the pressures were mounting to find the skiers, as fading light and falling temperatures would add further difficulties to an already challenging rescue. Heinrich kept close to Gretel as she scoured up and down the mountainside.

Nightfall took hold and the team switched on their powerful torches, scanning the slopes as they tracked Gretel's movements. Emerita's father had started to discuss with the team the possibility of calling off the search, as the weather forecast had predicted snowstorms for the next few hours, and resuming in the morning. The consequences on taking that decision would be three dead bodies. He could see the reports in all the papers and social media sources. *'Swiss search team fail to rescue French Ambassador's wife.'* The general consensus among the team was to hang on for another hour; the blizzard that was blowing up from Italy was not due for another hour or two.

Emerita nudged her father in the back. "Father, look." Gretel had stopped meandering all over the place and was actually circling around a small patch of snow fifty metres below where they stood; her tail was up, her nose buried in the snow, and she had started to paw at the ground. Gretel sat back and began barking, indicating to all she had found the cross-country skiers. For Gretel her job was done, but for everybody else theirs had just started.

The whole group slowly descended the mountain to where Heinrich and Gretel were stationed. The lighting equipment was set up, the helicopter that had returned to base had been recalled and instructed to land at the ski resort. Emerita shouted to the team to be silent. Her father looked at her in surprise, but ignoring his facial expressions she laid herself flat on the ground; she took a deep breath before yelling at the top of her voice, "Can you hear me?" She repeated the message several times, remembering to listen for a reply. Moments later the tip of a ski pole broke the surface of the snow. Heinrich quickly realised that the cross-country skiers were probably no more than a metre down. Emerita grabbed a spade; she was not going to be outdone by her brother and the other men around her. She knew that when you dig people out it was done in an orderly manner so as to ensure your actions did not cause further destruction of the scene, thus putting the lives of those being rescued and those doing the rescuing at greater risk.

Snow had started to fall and the wind was picking up speed; the storm was early. The team continued digging as this was going to be a race against time. At last they had broken through; the skiers where buried a little deeper than originally thought. Heinrich could see that two ski poles had been tied together to form a long pole that eventually ruptured the surface. The French party of skiers had been lucky, as they had managed to make it into a small cave before the wall of snow hit them; all three ladies appeared to be in good health apart from cuts and bruises and the onset of hypothermia. The French Ambassador's wife had sprained her ankle badly and was in considerable discomfort. The first two ladies were helped out and immediately wrapped in silver foil blankets for warmth. Emerita put her hands on two small plastic beakers, carefully pouring the brandy that was around Gretel's neck to warm the ladies up.

Further examination of the French Ambassador's wife by the team doctor revealed the damage was possibly more than a nasty sprain; he suspected she had a serious fracture. Carefully strapping her right leg and administering a small amount of morphine to ease the pain, he gave the all clear to go. Other members of the team climbed down to assist and, as gently as they could, they lifted the French Ambassador's wife to the surface; the pain was clearly visible on her face, yet she kept a dignified silence. The whole team had taken the decision that this lady should be flown direct to the nearest local hospital. With the helicopter hovering high above them and the stretcher securely harnessed to the winch, the doctor and his patient were hauled up to the helicopter. As they ascended the winds from the storm combined with the downdraft from the helicopter's blades caused the stretcher to swing violently around. The pilot had to draw on all his skills and expertise to keep the helicopter airborne and was relieved when the doctor and the French Ambassador's wife were securely on board. With the door firmly shut the helicopter departed down the valley.

The rescue team, delighted with the outcome, gathered their equipment with a sense of urgency, for the snow was now falling heavily and visibility was deteriorating fast. Emerita's father knew the mountain like the back of his hand and it was going to take all his experience to guide the team off the mountain and back to base. The two remaining survivors were roped to two members of the team for safety and support. Emerita had attached herself to her father. She was feeling very insecure at this precise moment.

The cable car ride back down the mountain was swift; the car itself was warm, which was welcome. Emerita looked at her phone; there was a message from her mother. *'Tell your father that I'm extremely annoyed with him for taking you up on a dangerous rescue, and I will be having words with him.'* Emerita tapped her father on the shoulder and showed him the message. He looked at her, shrugged his shoulders and simply said to her, "You have made me a very proud man. Don't worry about your mother, I'll get your brother to calm her down."

This had been an adventurous day for Emerita, from watching world dignitaries arriving at The World Economic Forum to rescuing a French Ambassador's wife trapped in an avalanche.

"What do you think caused the avalanche, Father?"

"Who knows, sweetheart."

"Is mother going to kill you?"

"Probably."

DANTEL

The orphanage in Arequipa was situated in the back streets. El Misti, the dormant volcano that dominated the skyline of Peru's second city, was visible from Dantel's room. The white, snow-capped peak dazzled against the clear azure blue sky, a normal summer's day for a city high in the Peruvian Andes.

Dantel knocked on Emilio's door; he was surprised when his brother didn't answer and merely assumed that he had left early to play football, as there was no school today with it being Saturday. The two brothers were very different in character; Dantel was the academic while Emilio was more of a sporty nature. The orphanage was unusually quiet for this time of the morning and Dantel couldn't understand why; nevertheless, he went back to his room to continue with his reading. He glanced at the photograph of his parents, which he kept on top of a small locker in the corner of his room. He distinctly remembered the day five years ago, when two heavily-armed men in full riot gear from the local Policia banged on their front door. With them was a small figure of a lady dressed as a nun; this was the first time he and Emilio met Mother Anastasia, whom they always referred to as Mother A from that day onwards. She sat them down and explained that their parents were involved with one of the street drug cartels and that there had been a skirmish in a nearby village with the Drug Enforcement Agency from Lima. The outcome was that their parents had been shot and had died of their injuries. They had been left as orphans. The orphanage, run by Mother A, had twelve children in it, all there as a result of the impact of parents or close relatives losing their lives as a result of drug-related issues.

Dantel texted his brother, '*Where are you? Did you feel that tremor?*'

'*Stop worrying Dantel, we often get the shakes, we live in an earthquake zone man. See you back at lunch, better still come down to watch me play, usual place, get some money from Mother A, then we can go to the café down by the monastery for lunch. Emilio.*'

Dantel knew precisely which café Emilio was referring to; they often went there after school to catch up with friends. The café was next to the Santa Catalina Monastery on Ugarte. If he ran he would be there in twenty minutes; cutting through the back streets and along the Rio Chili would shorten the journey. As he ran towards the Puente Bajo Grau Bridge that spanned the Rio Chili, the main river that flowed through Arequipa, his phone rang. It was Mayu, one of the older children from the home.

"Where are you, Dantel? Mother A is panicking; the social media websites and the local radio stations are warning people to leave the city because the tremors the city has experienced over the past few days are getting stronger. Where is Emilio?"

"He is with his football friends in the derelict yard next to the petrol station on Av La Marina."

"Mother A says for both of you to get back here now; she is packing the minibus in readiness to evacuate."

"Okay Mayu, we will be there shortly."

Dantel knew the drill as to what to do when an earthquake struck – head to a door or dash under the table or bed, whatever would break the fall of tumbling masonry. He also knew Emilio knew the procedure. The school and Mother A had taught them that the newly-constructed buildings were safer, as they had been designed to withstand the forces of a major earthquake, but the older, more traditional properties would collapse. Both of them knew the earthquake itself was not the main killer, but being crushed to death by old, poorly-built houses was.

The earthquake struck at 11.01am. Dantel reached for the street lamp and clung to it with all his physical strength; the ground to his left opened up and the noise of the land splitting apart was deafening. He could hear people screaming. Glass was showering down from upstairs windows, underground water pipes cracked, spilling water and sewage everywhere, gas pipes exploded; he watched the bridge that he was about to cross bend and twist until it finally snapped, sending cars and people downriver. The old buildings crumpled with ease, spilling their contents onto the surrounding streets; he could see people being buried alive under the falling brick and stonework that tumbled from the heavens. The street lamp he so desperately hung on to swayed violently as the ground continued ripping itself apart. An old wooden window frame struck him on the back of his head. The bang on the head caused Dantel to black out. He felt himself falling; as he fell he must have hit his head on hard stone, for when he woke up slightly dazed moments later he saw blood on his jacket sleeve where his head had come to rest. Dantel fumbled around the pavement looking for his phone. Still feeling light-headed, he got to his feet and saw his phone a few paces ahead. He reached down to pick it up, amazed it still worked. The time was 11.07am.

Looking around, the level of destruction was beyond belief. Six minutes ago everything was in perfect working order, but now all he could see was carnage. The last six minutes felt like an eternity but the ground had, for now, fallen silent. The aftershocks would come shortly, as they always did, and they would be as strong as the original quake. For now Dantel had to somehow find his ten-year-old brother in all this chaos.

The bridge had sustained quite a lot of damage; he needed to cross it to get to Emilio. For several minutes he stared across, mapping out the best route; people were screaming for help all around him, but he shut them out of his thoughts. Still slightly dazed, he picked his way through the strewn debris of twisted concrete; the iron rods that had been embedded into the concrete to strengthen it were sticking up all over the place. Their snapped, sharp edges would easily gash his legs; an injury was the last thing he wanted at this precise moment. The railing was surprisingly intact; using that as support, he managed to get three-quarters of the way across. The earthquake had sent the rest of the bridge tumbling into the river below. A small builders' merchants van abandoned by its owner was precariously balancing on the edge. Dantel carefully reached across; opening the back doors he saw a length of rope and, fastening one end to the railings, he shouted at a group of people that were standing at the far end of the bridge. "Catch." Moments later he had managed to scramble to the other side, thanking the people who had helped him as he raced off to where Emilio and his friends would be.

The city emergency services had started to respond to the situation; sirens could be heard going off throughout the streets. Reaching the old derelict yard next to the petrol station, Dantel could see that the old block of flats that had stood empty for years on the other side of the yard had collapsed, covering Emilio's football spot. Dantel stopped in his tracks; leaning against a wall he looked at the pile of rubble. Deep within his heart he knew Emilio and his friends were buried deep. Was Emilio dead, alive, hurt? He couldn't imagine, but he knew one thing; he had to get help.

Racing across the street, he ignored the man shouting at him from the petrol station. The man was trying to tell him and others that the petrol storage tanks underneath the pumps had been ruptured by the earthquake and were leaking. Dantel could smell the fumes; the spillage was clearly visible flowing down the street, but what Dantel had forgotten in his panic was the risk of a fireball explosion if the petrol ignited. Further along Av La Marina a small group of people had already flagged down a passing fire engine. Dantel saw them and sprinted; as he reached them he could feel his heart and lungs giving out with complete exhaustion. Collapsing at the feet of the firemen, he screamed for help. Within a few minutes he had regained his breath; apologising for his rudeness to the bystanders he promptly guided everybody to the collapsed building that had engulfed Emilio and his friends.

A spotty teenager who was standing by the Chief Fire Officer was surprised to get a text from one of his friends asking if he was alright; everybody assumed that the phone networks would have been put out of action, but apparently not. Dantel sent a message to Emilio, hoping and praying he would get a response. Everybody knew how to conduct a search; it had been drilled into them from their schooldays. The first few hours were vital. You worked in an organised manner, being careful as you lifted the rubble away. You worked as a team and you worked in silence so that you could listen out for voices calling out for help from below.

Dantel stood in line as the adults and fire crew had started to clear a small area directly in front of them. The Chief Fire Officer had taken charge of the site and made sure that as the fallen concrete and bricks were picked up and passed down the line of helpers their actions were not causing the collapsed building to collapse even further and potentially put lives at risk. Dantel was the youngest in the group, being twelve years of age, and as such was placed at the end of the line. It was his job to throw the rubble down the street out of harm's way. He was looking up the line when the phone in his trouser pocket pinged; reaching for his phone he quickly read the message that was on the screen.

'Dantel I'm alive. I think I have broken my left leg, it is trapped under a big block of concrete. I cannot feel my foot. I can see blood around my ankle from my torch on the phone. All of us are trapped under a large block of concrete. Get us out of here.'

'Where were you Emilio in the yard when the earthquake stuck?'

'We were at the far end furthest form the petrol station, near where all the graffiti is.'

'Emilio can you see any of the graffiti?'

'Yes.'

'Send me a snapshot of it.'

Dantel looked at the snapshot image; he knew exactly where that was.

'I know where that filthy graffiti is. I'm coming to get you. I have a rescue team on site now. I'm coming to get you bruv. X'

Dantel shouted at the others and showed the messages to the Chief Fire Officer.

The temperature in Arequipa had increased as the day progressed. The rescue team had put out requests for any construction companies that had diggers or drills to bring them to the site on Av La

Marina. Local TV companies had got hold of the story and had turned up. Reporters with camera crews were sending out up-to date live coverage of the rescue.

Dantel texted Emilio to tell him he and his friends were on national TV.

It was early evening before a digger was found; by now the heat of the day was starting to cool and the onset of the night sky meant that the floodlights, that had been given with a small generator, needed to be switched on. The earthquake had damaged the power lines to the city and, as night approached, Arequipa was plunged into darkness, making rescue operations difficult and dangerous. Aftershocks still shook the area, causing disruption to the search team as they would have to stop and take cover. Seven hours had passed and Emilio and his friends were still trapped underground. Dantel kept sending messages of hope; Emilio replied several times, but the last response Dantel had received from his brother was over an hour ago. He was beginning to get anxious; the rescue team assumed Emilio's phone had died and reassured Dantel they would get his brother out.

The digger had carefully removed layers of rubble. Dantel could sue the top of the graffiti; he knew they were only feet away. The Chief Fire Officer ordered the digger to stop; from now on they would use their hands to dig the boys out. Every five minutes Dantel shouted Emilio, followed by a moment of silence by everybody as they listened for a response. Dantel was getting tired and distraught; the day's events had exhausted him and Emilio wasn't responding. He kept on calling his brother and finally, twenty minutes later, a faint voice could be heard. Frantic hands kept tearing away at the earth. Dantel had all of a sudden found a new wave of energy; he tore at the ground and, a few minutes later, a small opening emerged. Through it a hand appeared, Dantel recognising it as Emilio's, for on the thumb was their father's wedding ring.

Dantel had done his work; he had found his brother and now it was up to the rescue team to finish the job off. The reporters and camera crews crowded around, one by one; as the small opening had been enlarged the boys emerged to cheers of jubilation from the waiting onlookers. Miraculously the boys escaped relatively unscathed, with only minor cuts and bruises to show for their ordeal. Dantel peered into the hole and he could see Emilio still trapped, his left leg caught under a large concrete block. The Chief Fire Officer took one look at Emilio's position; he had seen situations like this on several occasions and from the amount of blood Emilio was sitting in it did not look good. They would need to get a paramedic to Emilio to administer painkillers; once they started working around him to remove the concrete block the pain would become unbearable. All Dantel could do was talk to his brother as the rescue team worked through the rest of the night to free him.

In the early hours of morning Emilio was freed;

as his head appeared above the ground for the first time in eighteen hours, the large crowd that had spent the night sleeping in the open in fear of further aftershocks applauded. Mother A was there at the site, as she had been all night. Emilio was ushered into a nearby ambulance and while sitting in the back as the ambulance crew prepared Emilio for the short trip to the hospital, a message appeared on Dantel's phone. It was from the Peruvian President.

'I am so glad to see that both of you have survived this terrible earthquake. I cannot begin to imagine what you have been through. I was out of the country on a business trip when the earthquake struck our land. I am flying down this afternoon to Arequipa to see the damage for myself and what we need to do to repair your city. I have asked if I could come to visit you both in hospital. See you this afternoon.'

"How did the President get your number, Dantel?"

"No idea, bruv."

For Dantel the fact the President was coming to see them was exciting, but more importantly he still had his brother and both of them were alive. The brothers would never forget this day, but like most people they would learn to live with the occasional disasters; equally they would go on to enjoy the rest of their lives celebrating each other's achievements.

Dantel was grateful for the slight gap in the rubble that allowed his and Emilio's phone signals to connect that ultimately saved Emilio's life.

PRIYA

Priya was born on the outskirts of a small farming village near Khasa in the Punjab region of India. She was born blind to destitute parents that lived a hand to mouth existence. Life was harsh for the village children, as they would be expected to work to support the family. Being a girl, she held very little prestige in the community; her blindness, to some, was seen as a disgrace on the family. Her brothers and sisters were older and worked in the fields after school and integrated into the community, but Priya was very often shunned. At three she was left on the side of road with a small bundle of clothes; the family crops they had recently sown had failed due to the prolonged drought. With no work, the family were left with no choice but to up sticks. The note that was pinned to Priya's sari read: *'Take care of our daughter, whoever you are.'*

Nine years had passed since that fateful day and life for Priya had moved on. It was early in the morning and the beggars had already secured their pitches for the day. The temperature for early summer was already at thirty degrees and the streets were thronging with worshippers and tourists heading to the Temple complex. Amritsar is the centre of the Sikh religion, and at its heart lies the Harmandir Sahib, known to the world as The Golden Temple. The Temple came to the world's attention in 1984 when Indira Ghandi, the then Indian Prime Minister, gave orders for the Temple to be stormed in an attempt to control Punjabi insurgents. That decision to invade the holiest Sikh Temple resulted in her assassination on the 31St October 1984 by two of her Sikh bodyguards in the grounds of the Prime Minster's Gardens in the capital, New Delhi.

Priya never forgot the day she was left by the roadside; she often recalled the days she sat there calling out to passers-by for help, but being a blind impoverished girl from a low caste she held little value back then in Indian society. She remembered the gentle hand of a young New Zealand backpacker lady picking her up and carrying her here to Amritsar; the orphanage door being opened by a small group of children who, like herself, had been abandoned to the streets by their families. Each child had their own story to tell as to why they had been deserted; poverty and family issues were the main underlying factors in most cases.

The day was going to be busy. Her red embroidered bag was full of the tapestries she and her friends had made over the last few days; with all the worshippers and tourists out on the streets she was hoping to have a successful sales day. The door was open and most of the children from the orphanage had already left for the day. With her white stick in her right hand and her left hand on her best friend Neeta's right shoulder, she headed on her way. Priya had known Neeta for the last eight years and, being of a similar age and background, they had learnt to trust each other. They were more sisters than friends. Neeta stopped.

"Why have we stopped, Neeta?"

Standing on the step were two young ladies in their late teens, beautifully dressed in blue and purple saris. At first she didn't recognise their voices or their names, and it was only when they handed her to touch and feel a battered old rag doll with its right eye missing did she start to wonder whether the two ladies standing there were her older sisters, Wisah and Mana. Taking a small step toward them she reached to feel their faces; her hands softly followed the curves and outlines of each sister's facial features. Mana handed her a small gold bracelet that had an inscription on the outside; running her fingers over it, she immediately recognised it, as it had the names of all three sisters nicely engraved. Their grandmother, on her birth, had presented each of them with a gold bracelet bearing their names; she still had her bracelet in a drawer. The tears of emotion she had been fighting to hold back finally spilled over and poured down her cheeks; her sisters had returned.

It was mid-morning and the temperature had gone up to forty degrees. The short walk via the backstreets to The Golden Temple would take approximately twenty minutes. En route Wisah explained that they had not forgotten her and had spent years trying to find her.

"Priya, it was a friend of ours who had come to visit the temple; you sold her one of your little tapestries. She saw your bracelet with our names on, and she knew we had a blind sister called Priya whom we were desperate to find. She took a picture of you on Instagram. We immediately recognised the bracelet and have been in Amritsar for the last few days searching for you around the Temple. We showed numerous people the Instagram picture and yesterday afternoon a small group of children told us you worked as a volunteer in the soup kitchens. Last night we discreetly followed you home."

"Yes, Neeta and I go to the Langar everyday; we wash the soup bowls that are left over from the thousands of visitors that pass through the doors each day. Our pay is a free meal."

Being late today, the spot by the steps that led up to the Sikh Museum where Neeta and herself usually pitched themselves had gone. In the cut-throat business of touting your wares around the Temple complex, if you wanted the best pitch you needed to be in place early.

Nine years of street life had taught Priya to be streetwise and, despite being blind, she had learnt the hard way to be self-sufficient, a mini entrepreneur. She knew that to progress in life she would need an education, so the day a rich lady gave her a specially adapted laptop that was voice controlled and money to pay for computer classes was the day her political career started. To many that brushed by her each day she was simply a blind beggar girl; she couldn't see them but she could hear them. Listening to their conversations she knew where they had come from in the world and what they hoped to achieve. Did they stop to ask her what she wanted in life once they had purchased their little piece of tapestry bearing a sewn picture of The Golden Temple on? No. Did they care? No. Most of them were only concerned that the little tapestry piece they had bought for a couple of rupees would fit in their suitcase for the flight home.

With their main pitch taken, Priya and Neeta found an empty space outside one or the many shoe stores, where worshippers and tourists alike removed their shoes before washing their feet and entering the Temple. Neeta unfolded the yellow silk shawl, on which she and Priya placed their tapestries. The pavement was baking hot from being scorched by the overhead midday sun; Priya knelt down to feel for the edges of the shawl before tipping the contents of her red embroidered bag out. There was no point in creating a beautiful layout, as rummaging hands over the next few hours would have ruined the best of any display. The purpose was to sell the little tapestries, not show them off. The noise and the hustle and bustle from the surrounding streets was overwhelming for Wisah and Mana as they sat and watched their younger sister haggle with visitors. They were taken aback to see her fight and stand her ground amongst the scores of other children, all desperate to sell their knick-knacks for a couple of rupees. A good day in the eyes of the street children would be to have enough money for a bowl of rice and a small scrap of naan bread on the way home from the street vendors. If anything were left, those few remaining rupees would go to supporting their brothers and sisters.

Wisah was amazed by her younger sister's inner strength and ruthless determination here on the streets around the Temple; she bent down and picked up the yellow silk shawl carefully folding it before placing it in Priya's red embroidered bag. As she tied the bows securing the bag, she felt Priya's hand touch her left arm; looking up she could see Priya had something on her mind.

"Why did they leave me, Wisah?"

"Times were hard, Priya. The crops had failed, the rent hadn't been paid for months and the landlord had evicted us from the land."

"Where did you go?"

"We went to Delhi. Father got a job in a small hotel washing dishes, and Mother had several cleaning jobs."

"Where are my parents now?"

"Father died a few years ago; he had a stroke and never recovered. Mother lives with us in London."

"Hmmm…."

"Priya, we came back to look for you, but that little farming community we grew up in had gone. We asked the police and numerous nearby community elders for help. Months and years went by with no sighting of you, so after father's death we left for the UK."

"Why didn't they take me?"

"Priya, they could hardly support themselves. Father had heard that homes run by world leading charities took abandoned children with disabilities and that they were being fed and educated. He decided life for you would be better in one of those homes."

"So why didn't he and mother take me to one of those homes? They would have known where I was and how lonely and bereft I felt."

"Because, Priya, most of the homes were already overrun with orphans and would only take abandoned children. I understand how you feel…."

"You don't."

"If it's any consolation, Priya, mother has always kept a small photo of you in her purse."

"It's not! Why hasn't she come with you?"

"She doesn't know we are here. Mana and I wanted to make doubly sure that the girl in the Instagram photo was you."

"Hmmm…"

"Father did what he thought was best for you at the time, which was hard, I know."

'"You lot had value to them. You could go out to work and bring in money; pay your way. Me, I was a burden and had little value in their eyes."

"That's not true, Priya."

"Well it is to me! So you can tell your mother you have found me and I am making my own way in the world without her."

The money she and Neeta had made was tucked into a small gold silk pouch and discreetly hidden within the many folds of her sari. Her share of today's takings would pay for her computer class later that evening. The short walk to the Langar kitchens was brief, despite the streets around the Golden Temple thronging with thousands of people waiting to get into the complex. Hundreds of visiting guests were already seated, enjoying the customary lentil soup that had been prepared and was being served by numerous volunteers. For years Priya and Neeta had come in the afternoon to help wash up some of the thousands of soup bowls that were left. Their reward – a simple free meal. Some days it was the only meal they got. Mana and Wisah rolled up their sleeves to help Priya face hours of repetitive washing. Priya had the same spot every day; the layout was imprinted in her brain. Amidst all the commotion of the Langar kitchen and the noise coming from the bustling streets outside, where the rickshaws, cars and buses jostled alongside people and the sacred cows, Priya dreamed about her future and plotted a plan how she was going to achieve her goal.

The bowls kept on coming, and as they did Priya told her sisters about her dreams and aspirations to be a politician in New Delhi or an ambassador at the UN in New York, where she could become a world leader in championing the causes of disadvantaged women from developing countries, lifting them out of poverty to becoming women of influence and power. But she herself needed an education; the evening classes she attended for her computer skills she knew would not be enough, but that was all she could afford for the present time. She told Wisah and Mana about her adapted laptop a lady had given her, along with a small amount of money, but that money she had spent on surviving. She went on to tell her sisters how, at the end of her day, she would connect to the Internet back at the orphanage, lie in bed and download audio books and listen to stories. She would also get the news from around the world telling her what had happened that day. Her ultimate aim was to one day address the whole assembly at the UN and tell her story of how she rose from abject poverty to a woman of world influence, proving to mankind if you have the wish and the desire you can achieve what you set out to do.

Wisah and Mana simply listened and thought to themselves what a terrible mistake their father had made. There was nothing they could do to put that right, but they could help Priya in reaching her goals. But first they had to build back years of missing trust. That was going to take time.

The heat of the day had started to subside as evening approached. Priya asked her sisters if they would like to come with her to her evening computer classes: she would need one of them to support her as she walked to the local school. Normally one of the other children from the orphanage would accompany her there and back.

The orphanage, though busy, was considerably quieter than the Langar. The other children who lived there were eager to find out about Priya's sisters and pestered them to tell their story. Priya had taken some time out in her room to freshen up and pick up her laptop. Coming back downstairs, she could hear the commotion going on as her sisters were being bombarded with hundreds of quickfire questions. Mana accompanied Priya to the nearby school, leaving Wisah to cope with inquisitive children. Priya had changed into a different sari, the bright reds she had being wearing all day giving way to pale shades of delphinium blue and pastel pinks.

The computer class was in a small room in a nearby school. Mana noticed that none of the other students had a disability, which intrigued her as to why Priya had chosen to study with these guys. Priya had already sensed Mana's inner thoughts.

"Mana, I'm blind but I'm as good as these friends of mine on a computer. My laptop keyboard is designed to speak to me as I tap the various keys."

During a small break in the session Priya showed her friends the latest story she had written and put on Amazon for people to read or listen to. She checked her Amazon account to hear how much money she had made from the sale of her stories. Mana sat in silent awe; she and Wisah thought they had come to rescue a poor blind beggar of a girl off the streets of Amritsar who they considered to be their missing sister. This eye-opening performance from her younger sister today simply left her stunned.

With the evening class done, Priya packed her stuff away, taking Mana's right arm they walked home.

"I can sense your surprise, Mana; you thought

you and Wisah would find a pathetic blind beggar of a girl, but what you found was something else."

"Ohh… absolutely."

"Learn a lesson then. Never judge someone by what you see, judge them when you have taken the time to get to know them. Let's go to the Temple to say thank you for today and observe the procession."

"Why do you go to the Temple? You are a Hindu, not a Sikh,"

"I like to go, that is all."

The Golden Temple was beautifully lit up in the night sky; the upper half of the Temple wrapped in its gold coat shone like a beacon to the world. The waters of the sacred pool from which the Temple rose were serene and calm. Priya told Mana where to sit so she could get a good view of the procession, a nightly ritual carried out by the Temple authorities as the Guru Granth Sahib, the central holy book of Sikhism with its religious texts, is taken to the Akal Takht Sikh Parliament overnight. At precisely 4am the next morning the holy book is brought back and placed in the inner sanctum of The Harmandir Sahib, where the daily life cycle of the Sikh complex starts all over again.

For Priya, this was a life-changing day; she had found out why she was abandoned and that the only way forward was in forgiving her family by taking small steps in getting to know them but, more importantly, trust them again. Inwardly she was delighted to see her two sisters. She had shown them how resourceful and resilient she had become and what her aspirations for the future were. Deep down she knew that she would need them to achieve her goals and probably have to leave Amritsar and head for London to get the education she would need to become a world leader that straddled the world's stage. But she would only go if her friend Neeta went with her.

COMING UP

I really hope you enjoyed reading my last five characters; I enjoyed creating them and doing the research to give them some authenticity. As in *Great Rescues* the stories are fictional, with a hint of facts added to the background.

My next five characters are young teenagers who meet world famous leaders; so I would like to introduce you to *Ephraim, Duscha, Malaina, Yeshe* and *Juan.*

Ephraim is a Jewish boy from Jerusalem in Israel, who has just turned thirteen. In keeping with Jewish custom he celebrates his Bar Mitzvah. His friend Ameer is a Palestinian Arab, and the two of them demonstrate to the world that a Jew and an Arab can live side-by-side. Two American secret service agents call at their bread stall; the agents are in town protecting the US President, who is attending the state funeral of Shimon Peres, a former President and Prime Minister of Israel. The two boys are keen to tell the US President their story and hatch a plan to attract his attention. They successfully do this and are invited to The White House for private talks.

Duscha is from Yakutsk, a town deep in one of the coldest regions of Russia: Siberia. Her grandfather refused to serve in the Russian Military in WW2 and was imprisoned in one of the prison camps around Yakutsk. Having served his sentence, the family was not allowed to return to St Petersburg, so they stayed in Siberia working in the diamond mines. Duscha's grandmother was a former ballet dancer at Russia's most famous ballet company, 'The Bolshoi.' Duscha follows in her grandmother's footsteps and sets out to Moscow to join the famous ballet company and ends up meeting with The Russian President in her red shoes.

Malaina loves her Ice Hockey; she lives in Quebec City, the capital of the French-speaking Canadian province of Quebec. Her parents are divorced; her father is a wealthy businessman who spends most of his time travelling the world attending wine trade fairs promoting the wines his large vineyards produce. Her mother is an alcoholic and a street dropout, addicted to drugs; Malaina often finds her sleeping in shop doorways and on park benches. Trying to balance the issues she has with her parents with her dreams to become a national Ice Hockey champion are not easy. A few words of encouragement she gets from the Canadian Prime Minister inspire her to keep going.

Yeshe is a young Tibetan boy from a poor village on the Tibetan Plateau sent by his family to train as a Buddhist monk. Coming from a simple background to the modern city of Lhasa, with all its worldly attractions, is difficult for him. His teacher sends him to Dharamshala in northern India to hear the teachings direct from the Dalai Lama.

Juan is a little Chilean boy who lives in the capital Santiago. He is mad about football. His father works most of the week in the copper mines of northern Chile. With his father away a lot, this cheeky twelve-year-old rules the house giving his mother plenty of grief. His friends are always up to no good, but they have fun.

ACKNOWLEDGEMENTS

Alex Davis for all his tutoring, editing skills and patience.

Dave Pearson for his wonderful character illustrations.

Camilla Wright for the professional photo. The airbrushing worked. www.camillawrightphotograpghy.com

Pete Mugleston for his technical skills on the webpage. One of the best friends a guy could have

MESSAGE

To all my young teenagers that read these five short stories: thank you.

I hope you enjoy them. If there are any words you don't understand, ask someone or better still Google them.

CONTACT

Please feel free to let me know what you think to the stories.

Twitter: John Thomas Crowley @jtcrowley187

Website: www.jtcrowley.com

Facebook: Jtc Crowley

Printed in Great Britain
by Amazon